the RIDDLE

the RIDDLE

written by Neal Starkman
illustrated by Ellen Joy Sasaki

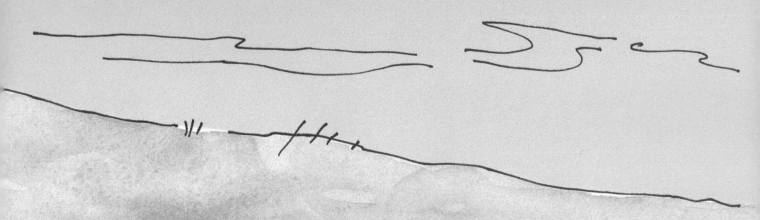

Library of Congress Cataloging-in-Publication Data
Starkman, Neal.
     The riddle / by Neal Starkman; illustrated by Ellen Joy Sasaki.
     Summary: When the second graders are assigned a riddle to solve, Maria pairs up
with the new student, Pete, and together they discover the answer to the riddle and
become friends.
     ISBN 0-935529-13-6
     [1. Friendship—Fiction.] I. Sasaki, Ellen, ill. II. Title.
     PZ7.S7955RI   1990
     (E)—dc20   89-25405
                                                                     CIP
                                                                  AC

To friends, and those still looking . . .

Maria was in the second grade. She had long black hair and a pretty smile. She was good at arithmetic, and she liked vanilla ice cream better than chocolate. Maria had a pet turtle named Slowpoke, and every once in awhile she would find a colored pebble to drop in Slowpoke's bowl.

One day Maria's teacher gave the class a riddle:

What can you make without using any tools?

What can you make without knowing any rules?

What can you make without planting any seeds?

What can you make that everyone needs?

8

"I want each of you to find somebody to work with," said Maria's teacher. "Try to answer the riddle by next week."

Everybody jumped up to find a partner. Maria had two good friends in class, Melanie and Rhonda. Which one should she choose?

Before she could decide, Maria saw Rhonda choose Melanie as a partner. She looked around the class. Everybody was choosing partners. Oh, no, she thought. Now I don't have any friends to be my partner.

Then she saw the new boy in class, the one who sat in the last row and didn't talk much. He was sitting in his chair and looking at his pencil. No one chose him for a partner. Maria looked around again for someone she knew, but everybody had been picked. Now what should I do, she thought.

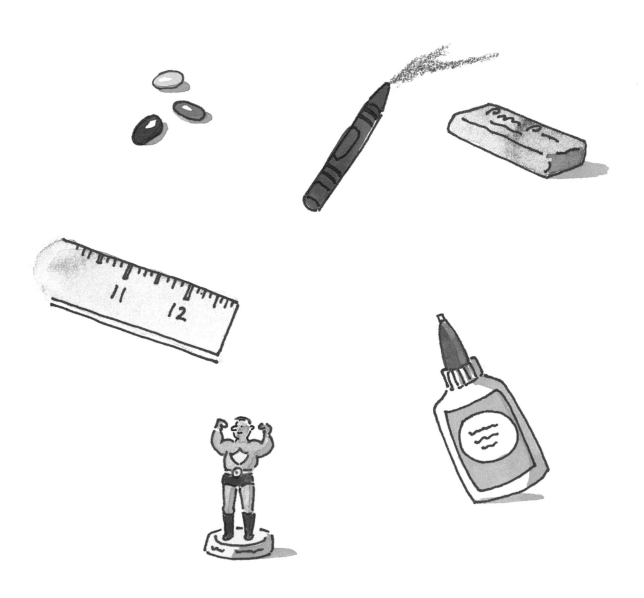

Maria took a deep breath and walked over to the new
boy. "Hi," she said. "I'm Maria." The boy gave a little jump.
"Hi," he said quietly, then went back to looking at his pencil.

Neither one said anything for a long time. "Well," Maria said, "would you like to work on the riddle with me?" The boy looked up again. "Okay," he said. "My name's Pete."

"Good," said Maria. "Let's talk about it at lunch."

"Okay," said Pete.

"I wrote down the riddle," said Maria, while she and Pete were eating their lunch.

"So did I," said Pete.

What can you make without using any tools?

What can you make without knowing any rules?

What can you make without planting any seeds?

What can you make that everyone needs?

"Well, what do you think?" asked Maria.

Pete was drinking his milk. "What about milk?" he said. "All you do is milk a cow. There aren't any tools, there aren't any rules, and there aren't any seeds! And everybody needs milk!"

Maria took a strand of her long hair in her hand and wrapped it around her finger. This is what she always did when she thought hard about something. "But doesn't a cow have to eat grass in order to give milk? You have to plant seeds to get grass."

"I thought grass grows wild," said Pete.

"No," said Maria, more sure now, "you need seeds. My grandma used to have beautiful gardens, and she planted seeds for grass to grow all around the garden."

"Okay," said Pete softly. "Hey, do you want to go on the swings?"

"Sure!" said Maria.

Maria was pushing Pete on the swings. "I guess," said Maria, "that you need tools to make swings." "Yes," said Pete. "Rules, too. You have to make sure that everything's the right length."

"How do you know that?" asked Maria.

"My dad's a carpenter. He's always figuring out stuff like that."

"Are you good at arithmetic?" asked Maria.

"Not that good. I don't know. I'm better at spelling."

"I'm good at arithmetic," said Maria. "I like playing with puzzles, too." Maria pushed Pete high on the swings, and he laughed. "Do you want to come over my house and play sometime?" asked Maria.

"Okay," said Pete.

"How about tomorrow?"

"I'll ask," said Pete.

Pete was showing Maria how to spell the word "friend" when Maria's mother brought in a big bowl of popcorn. "Thanks, Mom," said Maria. "Thank you," said Pete. He pointed to the popcorn. "Seeds, right?" Maria frowned. "Seeds? Oh, yeah, popcorn is made from seeds." She laughed.

The next day Maria's teacher gave the class a spelling
test. After class Maria was excited to see Pete. "I got an A!"
she said. "I got an A on my test!" Pete smiled. "Me, too. Hey!
Remember the riddle?"

What can you make without using any tools?
What can you make without knowing any rules?
What can you make without planting any seeds?
What can you make that everyone needs?

"You made an A. You didn't use any tools. You didn't know any rules. You didn't plant any seeds. Maybe that's the answer to the riddle!"

Maria thought about that. "No, I don't think so. There *are* rules for making an A on a test, like studying hard and getting a lot of sleep the night before."

"I guess so," said Pete. He frowned.

Maria looked at Pete. "Are you mad at me?"

Pete looked surprised. "Mad? No, I'm not mad at you, Maria."

"Well, sometimes when I tell you something you look like you're mad at me."

Pete shrugged. "I'm just not that smart, that's all. I'll never get the answer to this riddle."

"I think you're smart, Pete," said Maria. "You knew about the swings, and you helped me with my spelling."

Pete smiled. "I did, didn't I. Maybe I *am* smart!"
Maria laughed. "You're pretty funny," she said.

The next day Pete wasn't in school. Maria kept looking over at his empty desk. Maybe he's sick, she thought while reading her history book. He's probably got a cold.

In the afternoon, when everyone was eating lunch, Maria ate alone. Maybe his family moved away, she thought. Maybe they moved to France, and he wanted to leave me a note, but his father wouldn't let him, and they had to drag him into the car to go to France.

In the evening she was watching her favorite TV program, but she was thinking about Pete. Maybe, she thought, maybe he decided he didn't like me anymore and he ran away and joined a circus. Maybe he wanted to get a job as an acrobat, but they made him feed the lions, and at this very minute he's entering the cage of this really hungry lion. "How's your friend Pete?" asked Maria's mother. "What? My friend? Oh, I'm sure he's not afraid of any old lion," said Maria. Maria's mother shook her head.

The next day Maria got to class early, and watched the door as her friends came in. Finally, the teacher walked in-- and there was Pete! He didn't go to France, and he didn't join the circus! "Hi, Pete!" Maria called out. She waved at him. Pete smiled and waved back.

That Saturday Maria asked her mother if Pete could come to dinner. Maria's mother made hamburgers, salad, and re-fried beans. She smiled as Pete ate his food and kept looking at Maria. "Maria says that you're a pretty good speller. That's the first A she's ever made on a spelling test. You'll have to come over and help her again. Maria could use a friend like you."

Pete smiled and asked for more refried beans.

Later Maria and Pete were in Maria's room watching
Slowpoke the turtle eat *his* dinner.

"Have you thought about the riddle?" asked Maria.

> What can you make without using any tools?
> What can you make without knowing any rules?
> What can you make without planting any seeds?
> What can you make that everyone needs?

"I've thought about it," said Pete. "But everything I think of doesn't fit."

"Well, let's think some more," said Maria. "We have to have the answer by Monday. I know we can do it."

So Maria gave Pete a pencil and paper, and they came up with a list of things that they could make:

meatballs

cookies

spaghetti

funny noises

ice cream

footballs

rulers

airplanes

shoes

socks

the things
at the
ends of
your shoelaces

books

movies

hot dogs

Then, one by one, they crossed out all of them:

cookies   movies
airplanes   shoes
books   socks
rulers   shoelaces
hot dogs   the things at the ends
ice cream   of your shoelaces
spaghetti   funny noises
meatballs   footballs

"Maybe we'll think of something Monday morning," said Pete, but he said it in sort of a sad whisper.

"Even if we don't," said Maria, "let's meet after class."

"Okay," said Pete.

Maria sat at her desk, wrapping hair around her finger.
She had the riddle written in front of her:

What can you make without using any tools?

What can you make without knowing any rules?

What can you make without planting any seeds?

What can you make that everyone needs?

She really had hoped that she and Pete could solve the riddle. This past week had been so much fun. Well, even if they didn't solve the riddle, at least she had made a new—

Maria stopped playing with her hair. She turned around to look at Pete. He was looking at her and pointing at a sheet of paper on his desk. Of course, thought Maria. That's the answer! And Pete knows the answer, too!

"All of you sit next to your partners now," said Maria's teacher. Pete hurried over to where Maria was sitting.

"I know the answer to the riddle!" said Pete.

"Me, too!" said Maria.

"Does anyone know the answer to the riddle?" asked Maria's teacher.

Maria and Pete looked around the class. No one was raising hands. "We do!" said Maria and Pete together, and laughed.

"What is it?" asked the teacher. "What's the answer to the riddle?"

What can you make without using any tools?

What can you make without knowing any rules?

What can you make without planting any seeds?

What can you make that everyone needs?

"It's a **friend**!" said Maria. "Pete and I each made a friend this week! We played together, and we worked together, and I missed him when he was home sick one day, and we talked about different kinds of things, and he ate dinner at my house!"

"And we solved the riddle together," added Pete.

"That's the answer," said Maria's teacher. "*Everyone needs a friend.*"

Health Education Titles by
Comprehensive Health Education Foundation

The Apple
by Neal Starkman
the story of a teenager's two-year decline
into alcoholism, from his first drink to his
decision to get help, told in reverse chrono-
logical order
* *recommended for teenagers*

The Boy and the Hat
by Neal Starkman
a story in which a strange hat serves as a
metaphor for marijuana to illustrate the
harmful effects of this drug
* *recommended for children*

Don't Read This Book
by Neal Starkman
a book that challenges readers to become
more aware of themselves, to "think to
think," and to exercise independent
judgment
* *recommended for teenagers*

Face to Face
by Neal Starkman
a story about a teenage boy and girl who
must decide whether or not to have sex and
independently conclude that abstinence is
the best choice for them
* *recommended for teenagers*

The Forever Secret
by Neal Starkman
a journal of how a young person's experi-
ences with family, friends, and school are
affected by an alcoholic mother
* *recommended for children*

Martin the Cavebine
by Sara Nickerson
a story that provides young children with
an understanding and appreciation of
how people are unique and worthy of
consideration
* *recommended for children*

Personal Views
by Neal Starkman
an entertaining tale about a group of teenagers who learn what happens when they
judge people based on labels instead of
considering the whole person
* *recommended for teenagers*

Peter Parrot, Private Eye
by Sara Nickerson
the story of what Peter Parrot discovers
when he investigates why people drink, what
alcohol does to the body, and why children
should never drink alcohol
* *recommended for children*

The Quitters
by Neal Starkman
a story about three friends who learn
about the dangers of sidestream smoke
and experience different degrees of success
in attempting to get their family members
to stop smoking
* *recommended for children*

The Riddle
by Neal Starkman
a story about how a girl and boy become
friends without even knowing it as they
spend time together solving a riddle
* *recommended for children*

**The Roller Coaster: A Story of
Alcoholism and the Family**
by Don Fitzmahan
a story that helps children in alcoholic
families learn about their feelings and how
to express them
* *recommended for children*

Z's Gift
by Neal Starkman
the story of how a young boy responds to the
news that his teacher has AIDS and how he
teaches adults the meaning of compassion
* *recommended for children*

Large-Format Flip Books

(designed for reading aloud to a group of children)

A Girl Named Cherie
by Neal Starkman
a series of limericks describing what happens when a young girl tries alcohol for the first time
- *recommended for adults who work with children*

Max and the House Full of Poison
by Neal Starkman
a story about how Frog teaches his friend Max, a colorful blue gorilla, how a home can be poison-proofed for young children
- *recommended for adults who work with children*

The Roller Coaster: A Story of Alcoholism and the Family
by Don Fitzmahan
a story that helps children in alcoholic families learn about their feelings and how to express them
- *recommended for adults who work with children*

To order or to get more information:

AGC Educational Media
1560 Sherman Ave., Suite 100
Evanston, IL 60201
847-328-6700 or 800-323-9084